题献

She lends her pen,
to thoughts of him,
that flow from it,
in her solitary.

For she is his poet,
And he is her poetry.

她将她的笔，
借给她对他的想念，
思绪渗出笔尖，
在她的孤独中流淌。

因为她是他的诗人，
他是她的诗篇。

目录

◆ CONTENTS ◆

PART 1

不幸 ◆ MISADVENTURE

A Toast!

To new beginnings,
in fear and faith
and all it tinges.

To love is a dare,
when hope and despair,
are gates upon it hinges.

干杯！

为新的开始，
　　畏怯并坚定不移
　　就让一切蒙上惧色，让信念触染所有。

爱是孤注一掷，
　　当希望与绝望
　　成为它非此即彼的门扉。

XS AND OS

Love is a game
of tic-tac-toe,
constantly waiting,
for the next x or o.

X
与
O

爱是一场游戏，

是一字棋[♥]；

时时在等待，

等待下一手X、下一次O。

[♥]一字棋，即“井”字游戏。——本书均为译注。

A Dangerous Recipe

To love him
is something,
I hold highly
suspicious.

Like having something,
so very delicious—
then being told,
to do the dishes.

危险的美味

爱上他，
　　让我
　　每时每刻
　　心提胆吊。

好似品尝着珍馐玉肴，
　　如此美妙——
　　却被一声使唤，
　　难逃那满槽的锅碗盆瓢。

JUST FRIENDS

I know that I don't own you,
and perhaps I never will,
so my anger when you're with her,
I have no right to feel.

I know that you don't owe me,
and I shouldn't ask for more;
I shouldn't feel so let down,
all the times when you don't call.

What I feel—I shouldn't show you,
so when you're around I won't;
I know I've no right to feel it—
but it doesn't mean I don't.

只是朋友

我明了，我并不占据着你，
　　也许我永远无法做到，
　　所以，当你身处她的怀抱，那种怒恼，
　　我无权以之自扰。

我明了，你并不亏欠于我，
　　我不该再多奢求；
　　我不该那样失落——
　　当你不再提起听筒，电话静默。

我的感受，我不该向你透露，
　　所以，我不会开口，当你伴我左右；
　　我明了，我无权作此感受——
　　可我的感受，又岂是子虚乌有。

When Ignorance Is Bliss

I deplore,
being ignored.

For—

I am not a bore!

But it's perplexingly sweet,
and quite sexy too—
to be ignored,
ignored by you.

当「无知」是福

我哀声叹息，
　　当我承受漠然、被人忽视。

因为——

我绝非惹人讨厌的累赘！

可不知为何，那滋味竟甘甜如蜜
　　迷人、性感——
　　当我被你忽视，
　　承受你的漠然。

Heart on the Line

Love is good,
it is never bad—
but it will drive you mad!

When it is given to you,
in dribs and drabs.

心悬一线

爱始终美好
　　来者皆善——
　　却叫你情狂意乱！

当它任尔心焦，
　　滴滴点点、续续断断。

Sea of Strangers

In a sea of strangers,
you've longed to know me.
Your life spent sailing
to my shores.

The arms that yearn
to someday hold me,
will ache beneath
the heavy oars.

Please take your time
and take it slowly;
as all you do
will run its course.

And nothing else
can take what only—
was always meant
as solely yours.

陌生人的海洋

在陌生人的海洋，
　　你久久企盼，企盼与我相知。
　　你倾尽生命、乘风破浪，
　　驶向我的港湾。

那充满渴望的臂膀
　　只等有朝一日与我相拥，
　　疼痛在所难免，
　　当沉重的船桨高昂柄端。

愿你从容不迫，
　　何必匆匆；
　　只因你一切所为
　　都是理所当然。

没有任何人、任何事
　　能夺走那独独为你——
　　也永远为你注定的
　　非你莫属的彼岸。

Art and Books

Without a doubt,
I must read,
all the books
I've read about.

See the artworks
hung on hooks,
that I have only,
seen in books.

艺术与书籍

毫无疑问，
我必须阅读，
阅读所有
在书中读到的书。

也该亲眼看看艺术，
那些挂在墙上的，
我只在书中
见过的艺术。

A Voyage

To be guided
nor misguided
in love,
nor brokenhearted.

But to sail in waters—
uncharted.

航行

在爱情中
　　找到向导，
　　不入迷途，
　　不复心碎。

却要入海远航——
　　不问坐标。

A THANK-YOU NOTE

You have said
all the things
I need to hear
before I knew
I needed to hear them.

To be unafraid
of all the things
I used to fear,
before I knew
I shouldn't fear them.

感谢信

你说过
　　所有那些
　　我需要听到的话语——
　　在我明白
　　我需要听到它们之前。

不惧怕
　　任何一件
　　我曾经惧怕的东西——
　　在我明白
　　我不该惧怕它们之前。

AN ENDEARING TRAIT

The scatterbrain,
is a little like,
the patter of rain.

Neither here,
nor there,
but everywhere.

迷人的特质

那般心不在焉
似乎就像
轻快的雨点。

近不来，
远不待，
却无处不在。

His Word

I am not,
just a notch
on his belt.

What he feels for me,
he's never felt.

I am a word
he has heard
but has never seen
for himself.

Yet he wants to know,
how that word
is spelt.

他的话

我不仅仅
　　是他腰带上的
　　一个凹口。

对我，他唯有感觉，
　　没有感受。

我是一言一语
　　他已耳熟，
　　却不曾
　　亲眼领受。

可他总想猜透——
　　那只言片语
　　该如何拼凑。

A
WELL-DRESSED MAN

His charm
will disarm;
his smile,
in style;
his fashion,
in passion;
his words,
his flirt,
his tie
from his shirt,
to my wrists—
his kiss!
his kiss!
his kiss!

盛装先生

他的迷人
　　你欲罢不能；
　　他的微笑
　　造型独到；
　　他的时尚
　　热烈张扬；
　　他的言语，
　　他的情趣，
　　他系的领带
　　顺着他的衣衫
　　落在我的手腕——
　　他的嘴唇！
　　他的亲吻！
　　他的吻！

A Stranger

There is a love I reminisce,
like a seed
I've never sown.

Of lips that I am yet to kiss,
and eyes
not met my own.

Hands that wrap around my wrists,
and arms
that feel like home.

I wonder how it is I miss,
these things
I've never known.

陌生人

有一种爱，只在追忆中，
　　像一粒种子
　　不曾被我播种。

那副嘴唇，我不曾亲吻，
　　那对明眸
　　不曾与我的目光邂逅。

那双手，绕我的手腕一周，
　　那臂膀
　　似有家的温柔。

我不懂，我何以怀恋久久，
　　此间种种，
　　我从未亲身感受。

Wallflower

Shrinking in a corner,
pressed into the wall;
do they know I'm present,
am I here at all?

Is there a written rule book,
that tells you how to be—
all the right things to talk about—
that everyone has but me?

Slowly I am withering—
a flower deprived of sun;
longing to belong to—
somewhere or someone.

壁花姑娘

戚戚然，角落中，
　　屋墙紧，壁花熟；
　　我的存在，谁人注目？
　　莫非我——身在别处？

有没有写满规则的书卷，
　　关于如何存在——
　　和所有正确的言谈——
　　只有我无缘一看？

慢慢地，我在枯萎——
　　像花儿失去阳光；
　　久久的，我的念想——
　　想属于某个人、某个地方。

A Rollercoaster

You will find him in
my highs and lows;
in my mind,
he'll to and fro.

He's the tallest person,
that I know—
and so he keeps me,
on my toes.

过山车

他起起落落，
　　在我身边；
　　来来回回
　　在我心间。

他顶顶高拔，
　　无人比肩——
　　时时让我
　　踮起脚尖。

His Cause and Effect

He makes me turn,
he makes me toss;
his words mean mine
are at a loss.

He makes me blush!

He makes me want
to brush and floss.

「他的因果」

他让我翻来覆去，
　　辗转无眠；
　　一词一句，
　　我便难再多言。

他让我羞红了脸！

让我一心一念
　　想要牙刷牙线。

Lost and Found

A sunken chest,
on the ocean ground,
to never be found
was where he found me.

There he stirred,
my every thought,
my every word,
so gently, so profoundly.

Now I am kept,
from dreams I dreamt,
when once I slept,
so soundly.

失而复得

一副沉没的胸膛
在海底
深深隐藏；
那是他发现我的地方。

在那里，他轻轻唤起
我的一念一想、
一字一词，
那么温柔，那么深长。

如今，我远离
曾经的梦乡——
在那里，我久久酣睡，
那么安详。

AFRAID TO LOVE

I turn away
and close my heart—
to the promise of love
that is luring.

For the past has taught
to not be caught,
in what is not
worth pursuing—

To never do
the things I've done
that once had led
to my undoing.

怯不敢爱

我转身
挂上心锁——
拒绝爱的承诺，
远离诱惑。

因为曾经教会我
挣脱
一切不值得
陷入的旋涡——

不再让
相同的过错
重复
昨天的灾祸。

The Wanderer

What is she like?
I was told—
she is a
melancholy soul.

She is like
the sun to night;
a momentary gold.

A star when dimmed
by dawning light;
the flicker of
a candle blown.

A lonely kite
lost in flight—
someone once
had flown.

迷路的人

她是怎样的人？
　　我曾听闻——
　　她拥有
　　忧伤的灵魂。

她就像
　　夜晚的太阳，
　　灿烂了一瞬。

晨光中的星辰
　　黯淡了几分；
　　火光摇曳，
　　风吹灭了烛灯。

她是孤独的风筝，
　　飞不见，了无痕——
　　是谁的手
　　松开了线绳。

PART 2

忧伤马戏团

THE CIRCUS OF SORROWS

Circus Town

From a city so bright
to a strange little town;
on a carousel spinning,
around and around.

The dizzying height,
of the stars from the ground.

The world all alight—
with his sights, his sounds.

马戏小镇

从明亮的市城
　　到陌生的小镇；
　　坐着旋转的木马，
　　一圈圈奔腾。

在目眩的高空——
　　大地上撒满星辰。

世界灯火通明——
　　他的身影似火、声音如灯。

A Timeline

You and I
against a rule,
set for us by time.

A marker drawn
to show our end,
etched into its line.

The briefest moment
shared with you—
the longest
on my mind.

时光之线

时光定下规则，
　　摆在
　　你我面前。

它画下长线，
　　蚀刻成堑，
　　标记我们的终点。

你我之间
　　最短暂的重叠——
　　是我心中
　　最漫长的瞬间。

In Two Parts

You come and go so easily,
your life is as you knew—
while mine is split in two.

How I envy so the half of me,
who lived before love's due,
who was yet to know of you.

一分为二的人生

你来得轻易、走得从容，
你的日子如你所知，
我的生活只能从头。

我羡慕不已——那另一半的自己，
那时候，爱情犹可期，
不曾了解你。

A Bad Day

When thoughts of all but one,
are those I am keeping.

When sore though there is none,
for whom I am weeping.

A curtain drawn before the sun,
and I wish to go on sleeping.

糟糕的一天

当一切思绪如常，
　　独缺一个念想。

悲伤、苦楚，却别无一物
　　让我泪流成殇。

帘合窗前，不见阳光，
　　我只愿梦久眠长。

Rogue Planets

As a kid, I would count backwards from ten and imagine at one, there would be an explosion—perhaps caused by a rogue planet crashing into Earth or some other major catastrophe. When nothing happened, I'd feel relieved and at the same time, a little disappointed.

I think of you at ten; the first time I saw you. Your smile at nine and how it lit up something inside me I had thought long dead. Your lips at eight pressed against mine and at seven, your warm breath in my ear and your hands everywhere. You tell me you love me at six and at five we have our first real fight. At four we have our second and three, our third. At two you tell me you can't go on any longer and then at one, you ask me to stay.

And I am relieved, so relieved—and a little disappointed.

流浪的星球

小时候，我常会从十倒数，并想象数到一时会有爆炸一场——或因一颗流浪的行星撞上地球，或因别的什么奇灾异祸。最后，想象落空，一切如故，我便觉得安心，也不免有些失落。

数十的时候，我总会想起你，想起我们初次邂逅。数到九，我想起你的笑容，想起它如何点亮我灵魂深处的某种“死物”（当时我觉得它早已死掉）。数到八，我想起你的嘴唇，想起它们紧紧贴住我的嘴唇。数到七，你温暖的呼吸在我耳边，你的双手无处不在。数到六，你说你爱我，到五，我们第一次动了真格、闹得不可开交。数到四，我们第二次争吵。数到三，我们争吵再三。数到二，你说你已受够、无力再争个不休。数到一，你让我留下别走。

我觉得安心，那么安心——当然，也不免有些失落。

Closure

Like time suspended,
a wound unmended—
you and I.

We had no ending,
no said good-bye.

For all my life,
I'll wonder why.

终结

仿佛时间暂停、
　　伤痕未平——
　　在你我之间。

我们不曾到达终点，
　　没有一声再见。

只问其中缘由，千遍万遍，
　　在我余生之年。

A Question

It was a question I had worn on my lips for days—like a loose thread on my favorite sweater I couldn't resist pulling—despite knowing it could all unravel around me.

"Do you love me?" I ask.

In your hesitation I found my answer.

问题一种

一个问题，很多天，话在嘴边，只等开口——它就像我最心爱的毛衣上一个松脱的线头，我忍不住拉扯的冲动——尽管我明白一旦动手，只会衣散难收。

“你爱我吗？”我问。

在你的犹豫中，我找到了答案。

A WAY OUT

Do you know what it is like,
to lie in bed awake;
with thoughts to haunt
you every night,
of all your past mistakes.

Knowing sleep will set it right—
if you were not to wake.

逃离

你可知道，
　　卧床无眠，是怎样的感觉？
　　每天每夜，
　　回想连连，
　　关于曾经做错的一切。

我明白，一夕入梦便能安然释然——
　　如果永远不会醒来。

Lost Things

Do you know when you've lost something—like your favorite T-shirt or a set of keys—and while looking for it, you come across something else you once missed but have long since forgotten? Well whatever it was, there was a point where you decided to stop searching, maybe because it was no longer required or a new replacement was found. It is almost as if it never existed in the first place—until that moment of rediscovery, a flash of recognition.

Everyone has one—an inventory of lost things waiting to be found. Yearning to be acknowledged for the worth they once held in your life.

I think this is where I belong—among all your other lost things. A crumpled note at the bottom of a drawer or an old photograph pressed between the pages of a book. I hope someday you will find me and remember what I once meant to you.

失物

你知道吗？当你弄丢了某样东西（比如你最心爱的T恤，比如一串钥匙），四处寻找的时候，你常会在无意中找到那些你曾经弄丢、遗忘已久的东西。无论当初你丢了什么，总有那么一刻，你决定不再寻找；也许是因为你不再需要它了，也许是因为你找到了替代它的东西——它好像从一开始就不存在，直到你重新“发现”它，在一瞬间“认出”它来。

所有人都一样——都有一张“失物待寻”的清单；在列的每一件东西都渴望被承认：在你的生命中，它们曾经有过价值。

我想这就是我的归属——成为你的失物之一。像深埋屉底的一张皱巴巴的便笺，像夹在某本书里的一张黄旧的相片。我希望有一天你会找到我，想起曾经于你而言，我意味着什么。

A Betrayal

I cannot undo
what I have done;
I can't un-sing
a song that's sung.

And the saddest thing
about my regret—

I can't forgive me,
and you can't forget.

背叛

做过的事，
　　木已成舟；
　　唱过的歌，
　　覆水难收。

关于我的后悔，
　　最令人悲伤的是——

我无法原谅自己，
　　你无法彻底忘记。

AFTER YOU

If I wrote it in a book,
could I shelve it?

If I told of what you took,
would that help it?

If I will it,
can I un-feel it,
now I've felt it?

在你之后

我若把它写进书页，
　　可否在书橱里安放？

我若讲述你带走的一切，
　　是否会白忙一场？

如果我一意孤行，
　　此刻的心情、感想，
　　我能否统统忘光？

A REVERIE

A dusty room,
a window chair,
unseeing eyes
that gaze into
the montage of
a love affair.

A carousel
of memories,
spinning round
into a blur.

Her mind is now
a fairground ride—
she wonders if
you think of her.

幻想

一个落满灰尘的房间，
　　一张守在窗边的椅子，
　　视而未见的眼睛
　　凝视着
　　一场蒙太奇式的
　　爱情故事。

旋转的木马
　　搭载回忆，
　　转个不停，
　　模糊了光影。

她的内心
　　化作游乐之地——
　　她好奇
　　你是否会将她想起。

Letting Him Go

There is a particular kind of suffering to be experienced when you love something greater than yourself. A tender sacrifice.

Like the pained silence felt in the lost song of a mermaid; or the bent and broken feet of a dancing ballerina. It is in every considered step I am taking in the opposite direction of you.

给他自由

当你深爱着某种比你自己更重要的东西，就注定要承受某种特定的痛苦。那是一种温柔的牺牲——

就像美人鱼失落的歌声中那饱含悲恸的沉默，就像芭蕾演员曲足裂骨、翩翩起舞。我与你相背而行，每走一步都思虑再三，每走一步都承受着如此痛楚。

THE THINGS WE HIDE

And so,
I have put away
the photographs,
every trace of you
I know.

The things that seem
to matter less,
are the ones
we put on show.

我们的收藏

所以——

　　我已收起
　　那些照片，
　　所有我知道的
　　你的痕迹。

那些似乎

　　不再重要的回忆
　　成了我们
　　不停展示的东西。

Love Lost

There is one who you belong to,
whose love—there is no song for.
And though you know it's wrongful,
there is someone else you long for.

Your heart was once a vessel,
it was filled up to the brim;
until the day he left you,
now everything sings of him.

Of the two who came to love you,
to one, your heart you gave.
He lives in stars above you—
in the love who came and stayed.

失落的爱

一个人，成了你的归属，
他的爱，没有一支歌为之祝福；
你明白，一切都错得离谱，
却始终心在别处。

你曾心如杯斛，
盛满佳酿美酒。
直到那天，他独自远走；
世间所有，仍为他歌唱不休。

两个人先后到来，付出真爱；
只对其一，你把真心交代。
他以星辰为家，活在遥远的高空——
也活在那来而未走的爱情当中。

TIME TRAVELERS

In all our wrongs,
I want to write him,
in a time where
I can find him.

Before the tears
that tore us.

When our history was
before us.

时光旅人

在我们所有的过错里，
　　我想写信给他——
　　在我能
　　找到他的时间里。

在泪水
　　将我们撕裂之前。

当我们的故事
　　发生在我们相遇以前。

A Small Consolation

Everything that we once were,
is now a sad and lonely verse.

When once I had so much to say,
I am now bereft of words.

Sometimes it is the order of things,
that make them seem much worse.

It's not as if you would have stayed,
if I hadn't left you first.

小小的安慰

我们曾经的一切，
　　如今只是悲伤而孤独的诗篇。

从前我滔滔难绝，
　　如今却被剥夺了语言。

有时，是万物的定理
　　令寻常之事看似糟透。

即使我不曾放开你的手，
　　你也未必长留不走。

AN IMPOSSIBLE TASK

To try
or untry
to forget you not,
may be related
somewhat—

To tying,
then trying
to untie,
a complicated
knot.

不可能的任务

尝试
或放弃
不把你忘记，
多多少少
就像——

努力，
再努力，
去消解
一个“死缠乱打”的
绳结。

The Keeper

You were like a dream,
I wish I hadn't
slept through.

Within it I fell deeper,
than your heart would
care to let you.

I thought you were a keeper,
I wish I could
have kept you.

守护者

从前的你像一个梦，
我多希望
自己能长眠不复。

我在梦中坠落，
落向你的内心
不容你涉足的深处。

在我心中，你曾把一切守护，
我多希望
自己能将你守护。

Sad Songs

Once there was a boy who couldn't speak but owned a music box that held every song in all the world. One day he met a girl who had never heard a single melody in her entire life and so he played her his favorite song. He watched while her face lit up with wonder as the music filled the sky and the poetry of lyrics moved her in a way she had never felt before.

He would play his songs for her day after day and she would sit by him quietly—never seeming to mind that he could only speak to her through song. She loved everything he played for her, but of them all—she loved the sad songs best. So he began to play them more and more until eventually, sad songs were all she would hear.

One day, he noticed it had been a very long time since her last smile. When he asked her why, she took both his hands in hers and kissed them warmly. She thanked him for his gift of music and poetry but above all else—

for showing her sadness because she had known neither of these things before him. But it was now time for her to go away—to find someone who could show her what happiness was.

Do you remember the song that was playing the night we met?
No, but I remember every song I have heard since you left.

悲伤的歌

从前有一个男孩，他不能说话，却有一只能播放世间所有歌曲的音乐盒。有一天，他遇见一个女孩。女孩从没有听过音乐，不知“旋律”为何物。于是，他为女孩播放他最喜爱的歌曲。他久久望着女孩，只见她的脸上写满了惊奇；流淌的音乐填满了天空，诗般的歌词以一种前所未有的方式感动着她。

日复一日，男孩不停地为她播放，她则安静地坐在他身旁——男孩只能以歌声表达自己，可她丝毫不介意。男孩为她播放的每一首歌，她都爱听，可在所有歌里，那些悲伤的歌成了她的最爱。于是，男孩开始越来越多地播放那些曲目，直到最后——除了悲伤的歌，她什么也不爱听了。

有一天，他发现女孩已经很久很久没再露出过笑容。当他问起缘由，女孩握起他的双手，温柔地亲吻。

她感谢他，感谢他为她带来音乐、诗歌以及最重要的——感谢他让她了解了“悲伤”；因为在遇到他以前，她不知道什么是音乐，什么是诗歌，更不知道什么是悲伤。然而这时候，她也该走了——去寻找某个能让她了解“快乐”的人。

你还记得那天晚上，第一次见面时，我们听到的那首歌吗？

你不记得了吧。可我记得你离开以后我听过的每一首歌。

JEALOUSY

It was the way
you spoke about her.

With animosity, regret, disdain
and underneath it all—
just a hint of pride.

嫉妒

我忘不了
　　谈起她时你的腔调——

一切敌意、悔恨和鄙夷
　　都藏不住
　　那一丝骄傲。

Waking without You

Every song that sings of him,
from every heart
heard breaking.

I sing along in dreams of him,
I cling to—
when I start waking.

一个人醒来

每一首为他而唱的歌谣，
都发自内心，
伴随着每一颗心破碎的声音。

有他的梦里，我歌唱不停，
难舍难离——
当我开始梦醒。

That Day

I remember our highs in hues,
like the color of his eyes
as the sun was setting;
the pale of his hands in mine,
and the blue of his smile.

I remember our sorrows in shades,
like the gray of the shadows,
which loomed that day,
and the white in his lie
when he promised to stay.

那一天

我记得我们色调明亮的瞬间——
　　当太阳下山，
　　他双眸的色彩；
　　我手捧他双手的苍白，
　　看见他笑里透蓝[♥]。

我记得我们的悲伤染上阴霾；
　　那一天的阴影——
　　若隐若现地灰黯；
　　我记得他谎言中的纯白[♥]，
　　当他答应我不会离开。

♥蓝在英语中有“忧郁、忧伤”之意。
♥白色谎言（white lie）在英语中一般指“善意的谎言”。

The Girl He Loves

There was a man who I once knew,
for me there was no other.
The closer to loving me he grew,
the more he would grow further.

I tried to love him as his friend,
then to love him as his lover;
but he never loved me in the end—
his heart was for another.

他爱的女孩

曾经，我认识一个人，
没了他，我孑然一身。
渐渐地，他几乎爱上了我，
慢慢地，他也变得陌生。

我尝试，像朋友一样爱他，
再寻求爱人的身份；
可最终，他从未有爱于我——
他心里，住着另一个人。

A Lover's Past

The turbulent turns
and the tides
that twist them.

When what they once were,
was how she
had wished them.

And all the joys he brought her,
how she could
list them.

In time she will learn,
not to
miss them.

恋人故事

潮水阵阵，
　　扭曲了岸滩，
　　让激流转弯。

他们的美满
　　不负她
　　曾经的期盼。

他带来的所有快乐，
　　她早已
　　心中了然。

有一天她会明白，
　　错过了，
　　就为时已晚。

Beauty's Curse

Her bow is drawn
to worlds of dark;
where arrows spring
and miss their mark.

She'll turn their heads—
but not their hearts.

美的诅咒

她拉动弓弦，
　　身陷黑暗的境地；
　　在那里，万箭离弦，
　　无一中的。

她能改变箭的方向——
　　却无法改变它们的向往。

Dead Butterflies

I sometimes think about the fragility of glass—of broken shards tearing against soft skin. When in truth, it is the transparency that kills you. The pain of seeing through to something you can never quite touch.

For years I've kept you in secret, behind a glass screen. I've watched helplessly as day after day, your new girlfriend becomes your wife and then later, the mother of your children. Then realizing the irony in thinking you were the one under glass when in fact it has been me—a pinned butterfly—static and unmoving, watching while your other life unfolds.

死去的蝴蝶

我时而会想起玻璃的脆弱——想象碎片的边缘划过柔软的肌肤。而事实上，真正让你窒息的，是那种透明感——那种人物异侧，看得清却摸不着的痛苦。

年复一年，我把你当成我的秘密，把你置于玻璃屏下。日复一日，我无助地望着你，眼睁睁地看着你另结新欢，看着她变成你的妻子，看着她不多久就成了你孩子的母亲。接着，我意识到是我一厢情愿地以为玻璃下的人是你，多么讽刺——一直待在玻璃下的人是我才对，我才是那只被死死钉住的蝴蝶标本——一动不动、痴痴凝望，望着另一侧的你过上新的生活。

WISHFUL THINKING

You say that you are over me,
my heart—
it skips,
it sinks.

I see you now with someone new,
I stare,
I stare,
I blink.

Someday I'll be over you,
I know,
I know—
I think.

痴心妄想

你说你已不再想我，
　　我的心——
　　惊而又跳
　　下沉不停。

如今你已心有所属，我的目光
　　如注、
　　如凝，
　　忍不住眨了眨眼睛。

终有一天，我将不再想你，
　　是的，
　　我想我——
　　心知肚明。

A Heavy Heart

All you have done,
I had hoped to pardon.

When the death of love
was slow for me—
for you was sudden.

Now the years go by,
and my heart
has hardened.

沉重的心

你的过错，
　　我曾想一一宽免。

于我而言，
　　爱死得缓慢——
　　于你，却是突然之间。

彼时经年，
　　我的心冷而弥坚，
　　不复从前。

Saving You

The darkness takes him over,
the sickness pulls him in;
his eyes—a blown-out candle;
I wish to go with him.

Sometimes I see a flicker—
a light that shone from them;
I hold him to me tightly,
before he's gone again.

拯救

他落入黑暗之手，
　　难逃病魔之口；
　　他的双眸——好似熄灭的烛灯；
　　我多想伴他左右。

时而，我看见微亮闪动——
　　光芒一束，出自他的眼中；
　　紧紧地，我将他拥抱，
　　只怕他再次远走。

An Answer

To choose from
there were many;
among them,
there were some.

And of those I loved you,
more than any—
but not as much
as one.

回答

选择
　　要多不少；
　　或多或少
　　能如你所好。

我选择你，爱上你，
　　爱得无可比拟——
　　唯独一人
　　我难以企及。

Swan Song

Her heart is played
like well-worn strings;
in her eyes,
the sadness sings—
of one who was destined
for better things.

天鹅之歌♥

她的心声
　　像旧损的琴弦鸣响；
　　她看见
　　悲伤在歌唱——
　　为那个注定要离开、
　　注定会幸福的人歌唱。

♥天鹅之歌常用于形容天鹅临死前的哀鸣，也常用于比喻艺术家最后的作品或演出，可译为“绝响”。

PART 3

爱 ◆ LOVE

First Love

Before I fell
in love with words,
with setting skies
and singing birds—
it was you I fell
in love with first.

初恋

当我尚未
　　爱上辞藻、
　　爱上黄昏的天空
　　和歌唱的飞鸟——
　　你才是我
　　最初的美好。

He and I

When words run dry,
he does not try,
nor do I.

We are on par.

He just is,
I just am,
and we just are.

他和我

当言语变得苍白，
　　他陷入无奈，
　　我也不再辩白。

我们难分高下。

他就是他，
　　我就是我，
　　我们之间，又何来变化。

SUNDAYS WITH MICHAEL

I hold my breath and count to ten,
I stand and sit, then stand again.
I cross and then uncross my legs,
the planes are flying overhead.

The dial turns with every twist,
around the watch, around his wrist.
Resting there with pen in hand,
who could ever understand?

The way he writes of all I dream,
things kind yet cruel and in-between,
where underneath those twisted trees,
a pretty girl fallen to her knees.

Who could know the world we've spun?
I shrug my shoulders and hold my tongue.
I hold my breath and count to ten,
I stand and sit, then stand again.

和迈克尔在一起的星期天

我屏住呼吸，默数到十，
一起一坐，又复站起。
我叠起双腿，又复松离，
架架飞机，飞过天际。

那只手表，绕他手腕一周，
时针顿走，绕着表盘一周；
笔在手中，他的手一动不动，
谁又真正能懂？

他以他的方式，记下我所有的梦，
所有看似残酷、依旧模糊的事物，
在那扭曲的怪树下，
一个美丽的姑娘双膝落地，久久跪下。

谁人了解，我们编织的世界？
我轻轻耸肩，不发一言，
我再次屏住呼吸，默数到十，
一起一坐，又复站起。

Mornings with You

I slowly wake
as day is dawning,
to fingertips
and lips imploring.

The sheets against my skin,
he says,
like wrapping paper
on Christmas morning.

有你的清晨

天渐渐泛白，
　　我慢慢醒来，
　　感到指尖的触碰
　　和唇间的迫不及待。

他说，
　　紧绕我肌肤的床单，
　　就像层层的包裹——
　　在清晨的圣诞。

SOUL MATES

I don't know how you are so familiar to me—or why it feels less like I am getting to know you and more as though I am remembering who you are. How every smile, every whisper brings me closer to the impossible conclusion that I have known you before, I have loved you before—in another time, a different place—some other existence.

灵魂伴侣

我不知道，为什么在我眼中，你如此熟悉——或者说，我不知道，为什么我并不那么强烈地感受到自己正在慢慢地了解你——恰恰相反，我更像是在慢慢地想起你。我不知道，为什么那一次次微笑、一声声低语，无一不让我更加确信，确信一个不可能的结论：我曾认得你，也曾爱过你——在另一个时空，在不同的地点——以另一种存在的方式。

A Fairy Tale

Start of spring;
heart in bloom;
our whisperings
in sunlit rooms.

Summer was felt
a little more;
in autumn I
began to fall.

When winter came
with all its white,
you were mine
to kiss goodnight.

童话故事

春天到来，
　　心花盛开；
　　在洒满阳光的房间，
　　我们细语轻谈。

夏天的感觉
　　只留一丝余多；
　　秋天的我，
　　开始坠落。

冬日无痕，
　　纯白了世间千万；
　　我只把你亲吻，
　　祝你晚安。

ALWAYS

You were you,
and I was I;
we were two
before our time.

I was yours
before I knew,
and you have always
been mine too.

一直

曾经，你就是你，
　　我就是我，
　　只有你我二人，
　　没有我们。

不知不觉，
　　我已非你莫属；
　　你也一直
　　非我莫属。

A Dream

As the Earth began spinning faster and faster, we floated upwards, hands locked tightly together, eyes sad and bewildered. We watched as our faces grew younger and realized the Earth was spinning in reverse, moving us backwards in time.

Then we reached a point where I no longer knew who you were and I was grasping the hands of a stranger. But I didn't let go. And neither did you.

I had my first dream about you last night.
Really? She smiles. What was it about?
I don't remember exactly, but the whole time I was dreaming, I knew you were mine.

梦

当地球以越来越快的速度旋转，我们浮向空中，十指紧扣，困惑的眼眸中满是哀愁。我们久久凝视，发现彼此的面孔渐渐年轻，继而意识到地球正逆向转动，将我们送回曾经。

接着，我们回到原点，我再也认不出你，却仍紧紧抓住那双陌生的手。但我五指紧扣，你也不曾放手。

昨晚，我第一次梦见了你。

真的吗？她笑了。梦见什么？

记不清了，可在梦里，由始至终，我都清楚地知道：你属于我。

Before There Was You

When I used to look above,
all I saw was sky;
and every song
that I would sing,
I sung not knowing why.

All I thought and all I felt,
was only just because,
never was it ever you—
until it was all there was.

在你出现以前

从前，我抬起头，
　　望见的只有天空；
　　每一首
　　唱起的歌，
　　我都不知缘由。

我所有的念想与感受，
　　无非是念则成想、有感而受，
　　你不曾成为理由——
　　一切都可无可有。

BEAUTIFUL

Your hand reaches for mine.
We kiss tentatively, passionately
and then, tenderly.

You brush my hair away from my face.
"You're beautiful."
I wrinkle my nose in protest.
"You are."

美丽

你伸手寻找我的手。
　　我们彼此亲吻——陌生，热烈，
　　继而陷入温柔。

你伸手拨开我的头发。
　　“你真美。”
　　我鼻间一皱，故作执拗。
　　“真的很美。”

ALL OR NOTHING

If you love me
for what you see,
only your eyes would be
in love with me.

If you love me
for what you've heard,
then you would love me
for my words.

If you love
my heart and mind,
then you would love me,
for all that I'm.

But if you don't love
my every flaw,
then you mustn't love me—
not at all.

孤注一掷

若你爱的
是你看见的我，
那么爱着我的
只是你的眼睛。

若你爱的
是你听见的我，
那么我所说的
也能让你爱我。

若你爱的
是我的心灵和思想，
那么我的一切
都会让你爱我。

可若你不爱
我的每一个缺点，
那么你不该爱我——
绝不该爱我。

SOME TIME OUT

The time may not
be prime for us,
though you are
a special person.

We may be just
two different clocks,
that do not tock,
in unison.

戏外时光

时间也许
　　不曾善待我们，
　　尽管你是
　　特殊的人。

我们也许
　　是不同的时钟两台，
　　不共嘀嗒，
　　不同节拍。

Souls

When two souls fall in love, there is nothing else but the yearning to be close to the other. The presence that is felt through a hand held, a voice heard, or a smile seen.

Souls do not have calendars or clocks, nor do they understand the notion of time or distance. They only know it feels right to be with one another.

This is the reason why you miss someone so much when they are not there—even if they are only in the very next room. Your soul only feels their absence—it doesn't realize the separation is temporary.

Can I ask you something?
Anything.
Why is it every time we say good night, it feels like good-bye?

灵魂

当灵魂爱上彼此，万事皆休，只剩彼此接近的渴望——它存在，当十指紧扣，透过一丝声音，一抹笑容，便能感受。

灵魂不谙历法，不计分秒，分不清短暂、长久，不明了咫尺、远遥。只有彼此相依的美妙，它们知道。

所以，当它们不在身边，你会如此想念——即便它们就在隔壁的房间。你的灵魂，它唯独感受不到对方的存在——它不明白，何为暂时分开。

问个问题可好？

当然。

为什么我们的每一声晚安，听起来都像再见？

Solo Show

He pulls the thick woolen sweater
up, over my head.

Little sparks of static
dance across my skin.

Does it hurt? He says, running his hands
gently over my warm body.

It is your own little fireworks show,
I whisper.

单人秀

他拉起我厚厚的毛衣，
　　拉过我的头顶。

静电的火星点点
　　像落遍我肌肤的舞步。

疼吗？他边问边用双手
　　温柔地抚过我温热的身体。

这是你一个人的烟火表演，
　　我轻声回答。

THE FEAR OF LOSING YOU

Without meaning to,
he's disarmed me,
with kisses that soothe
and alarm me.

In arms that terrify
and calm me.

害怕失去你

不经意间，
　　你卸下我的防备，
　　你的吻将我抚慰，
　　也让我惊惴。

我依偎着，那让我胆怯、
　　也让我安心的手臂。

Ebb and Flow

She yearns to learn
how his tide is turned,
to understand
each grain of sand,
he knows.

To move in rhythm,
with his ebb and flow.

潮起潮落

她渴望着，想知道
　　他何以心潮反复，
　　想明了
　　每一粒
　　他熟悉的沙土。

渴望随他潮起潮落，
　　同心同步。

WRITTEN IN TRAFFIC

A quiet gladness,
in the busy sadness;
inside the final tussle,
of love and its madness.

Its goodness and badness,
its hustle and bustle.

写在车水马龙间

一份安静的喜悦
　　在纷繁的悲伤中，
　　在爱情最后的角逐
　　与疯狂中——

在它的是是非非、
　　熙熙攘攘之中。

ANGELS

It happens like this. One day you meet someone and for some inexplicable reason, you feel more connected to this stranger than anyone else—closer to them than your closest family. Perhaps because this person carries an angel within them—one sent to you for some higher purpose, to teach you an important lesson or to keep you safe during a perilous time. What you must do is trust in them—even if they come hand in hand with pain or suffering—the reason for their presence will become clear in due time.

Though here is a word of warning—you may grow to love this person but remember they are not yours to keep. Their purpose isn't to save you but to show you how to save yourself. And once this is fulfilled, the halo lifts and the angel leaves their body as the person exits your life. They will be a stranger to you once more..

It's so dark right now, I can't see any light around me.
That's because the light is coming from you. You can't see it but everyone else can.

天使

一切大概如此：

有一天，你遇见某个人，然后莫名其妙地，你觉得自己与眼前的陌生人紧密相连，无可比拟的紧密——超乎血缘之亲的亲近。或许，在他的身体里住着一位天使——上帝派来的天使，为了某个更高的目标，为了教给你重要一课，抑或保护你安然度过危险的时期。对他，你必须相信——即使痛苦与煎熬随之而来；到了恰当的时候，你自会明白他存在的理由。

不过在此，且留一声警告：

你也许会爱上此人，但请记住，你无法将他占为己有。他的出现，并不是为了把你拯救，而是为了让你懂得如何去把自己拯救。一旦目标达成，光晕便升入高空，他退出你的生活，天使也离开他的身体。他将再次变得陌生。

此时此刻，好黑、好暗，我的周围，看不见半点光亮。

看不见是因为光芒来自于你。可除了你，谁都能看见。

Golden Cage

A bird who hurt her wing,
now forgotten how to fly.

A song she used to sing,
but can't remember why.

A breath she caught and kept—
that left her in a sigh.

It hurts her so to love you,
but she won't say good-bye.

金笼

她是折翼的飞鸟，
忘了如何飞翔。

从前熟悉的歌谣，
不知为何唱响。

忽而聚敛的气息
只化作一袭长叹。

爱你她伤痕累累
却不说一声再见。

Love Letters

Every letter
that she types,
every keystroke
that she strikes—

To spell your name
again and again—
is all she ever
wants to write.

情书

每一封
　　她写下的信，
　　每一个
　　她敲下的键——

一次次
　　拼出你的名字——
　　是她想要
　　写下的一切。

CODEPENDENCY

There is nothing more nice,
there is nothing much worser;
than me as your vice
and you as my versa.

依赖

再好不过，
也再坏不过——
当你我之间，
“反之亦然”。

Canyons

*Rarely do the words **I love you** precede a question mark—but it is a question nonetheless and your answer to mine was the incarnation of a wish—the fulfillment of a promise.*

Somewhere between falling in and out of love, the question spilled from our lips over and over—readily answered with greedy hands and ravenous mouths. It was cautiously whispered on rooftops, as we looked down on terrifying heights and cried out under creased, white sheets in breathless admissions.

Towards good-bye, I asked the question and your reply was a thoughtless echo as I stood, feeling as though I was shouting meaningless words into an empty canyon—just to hear them repeated back.

***I love you,** he says for the first time.*
*I turn my body to face his. **Say it again.***
He says it over and over again, pulling me beneath him.

峡谷

我爱你这三个字，很少以问号收尾——可**我爱你**却无疑是个问题；你的回答是一个心愿的化身——一次承诺的完成。

从爱情开始到结束——之间的某个地带，这个问题不断从我们的唇间溢出——贪婪的双手和迫不及待的双唇伴随着一声声轻而易举的回答。当我们站在屋顶，从骇人的高处俯望，它化作谨慎的低语；在满是褶皱的白色被单下，在我们急促的呼吸间，它成了坦白似的吟叹。

说出再见以前，我以这三个字问你，你的回答如同不假思索的回声；我站在原地，仿佛对着空空的峡谷喊出毫无意义的字句——只听它们徒劳而返。

我爱你，他第一次对我说。

我转过身子，面对他。**再说一遍**。

他一遍又一遍地重复着，将我压在身下。

A TIME CAPSULE

This is where,
I began to care,
where I was befriended.

This is where,
my soul was bared,
where all my rules were bended.

This is where,
a moment we shared,
was stolen and expended.

Now this is where,
this is where,
this is where we've ended—

时空胶囊

此时此地，
　　我开始在意，
　　在我沦为朋友的今天。

此时此地，
　　我的灵魂失去护庇，
　　一身原则尽皆弯斜。

此时此地，
　　我们短暂的回忆
　　悄然失窃、终告耗竭。

就在此时
　　此地，
　　在这里，我们走到终点——

——情书

星期天，河畔公园，没有风，鸟儿困在树上，不停鸣啭，阳光刺眼，河面上没有一条船。人们在树荫下，在浓稠的安静中窃窃私语，不时露出他们的身体不再需要的浅笑。太阳一动不动，燃烧着夜的回忆，投下炽热的注视；你说，世上怎有不用翅膀、不系线绳便能在空中停留的东西——更可恶的是，你还看不清它的模样——虽然它赐予我们温暖与光亮。我们沿着河边的卵石路一直走，一直默然，青绿色的河面映出扭曲的倒影，分不清哪个是我，哪个是你；时光中，它们倾斜、轻颤，似是我们心中的千言万语。

偶然的微风。你微微上扬嘴角，仿佛突然想起了昨夜的梦。早些时候，你说梦里你一直在等待，等着风捎来星星的消息，可电话铃声把你吵醒，你喘着气，吸吮舌间的苦涩，裹紧了被汗水浸透的被单。你问我，我们是

它们抬起
又放下
疲惫的翅膀
竭尽全力
却仍困在地上

太阳高升
像不系线绳的风筝

屋里，他的声音
仿佛墙上的阴影。

他以星辰为家，
活在遥远的高空——
也活在那来而未走的
爱情当中。

今天见面吗，我不知该如何回答。

“等我一下。”

你捧起挂在前胸的宝丽来相机，轻盈地跑开，我莫名地感到嫉妒，目光却始终被你一身的纯白牢牢吸引。我拿出钱夹，取出第一次见面时你送我的照片：白色的衬衣，白色的表带，白色的长裙，白色的皮鞋。我指尖的汗液在你身上留下转瞬即逝的痕迹，十年前的你——十年，十年的忧愁在一瞬间蒸发，只把你不变的笑容和无数我无从知道的答案留下。

……你的声音渐飘渐远，像一张褪色的宝丽来相片。……一切似在昨天。

……无从了解的苦痛，我不会让你承受。

抬起头，已不见你的身影。我抬手想看手表——习惯仍在，却忘了不知从何时起，我已把时间置之度外，让回忆的胶片暂停。

她把时间置之度外，
所以，她永远解开了表带。

海，眼泪的故乡。阴天，它的嘈杂颠覆了我的想象。你回头凝望远去的海滩，风吹起你的头发，你眯起的眼睛模糊了笑意，乌黑的海鸟滑翔而过，在海平线消失，引擎在嘶吼，似是至纯的盐撒在了伤口，放肆的白浪如脓，张开大口，似要将流浪的心吞噬。

……一头乌黑的头发被海风吹乱，细薄的双唇微微上扬，浅笑中欣悦如沁。在他的生命中，她是独一无二的存在。

——没有漂流的瓶子。

……你是一只在大洋中漂流的瓶子。……每一次站在海边，我都会寻找你的身影。

我动动手脚，不让潜水衣粘上我的肤肉。它像一层没有解答的谜，像你的冷漠，它被海水浸透，牢固、沉重，镶满了细小的沙粒——陌生却又熟悉。我伸手抚摸你停在膝头的手背，像在试探往事的结界，可你没有回头。你说你曾深爱，你说你看到了朝思暮想的巨鲸，可那个人深如大海，鲸鱼悦耳的歌声中，尽是海的沉默。

想明了
每一粒
他熟悉的沙土

……就像美人鱼失落的歌声中那饱含悲恸的沉默……

你把脚心按在我的脚背，胶鞋阻隔了温度。天亮了一些，海水变得清澈，可身上这一层橡胶却给予我更深的容器感。橡胶下是我，我的身体里是什么？我心中的犹豫，是因为重生的渴望吗？

……不论我们将自己注入何等容器，如今我已生意满盈、活力四溢。我不断地超越，成为崭新的自己。

大雨倾盆，人群四散，我站在剧院门口，从衬衣口袋里掏出票根。

——《天鹅之舞》。

天鹅之歌

你说你不想再做伴舞，只想把舞台占为己有，因为在音乐里，在跃动的纯白间，你始终不知道自己身在何处。可你又说，每每独自跳舞，你已看不见梦中的天鹅，世界一片空白，因为你把爱都给了我。

他问我：你写诗，是为了什么？
我回答：为了把对你的爱献给世界。
因为你不要我的爱。

我多想冲进更衣间，把你看个明白；我不想变成你的观众，不想眼睁睁地看着你演绎他人的故事，我想站在你的位置，成为你的眼睛，把我自己看透，我想我们赤身裸体，不留缝隙地融合在一起。

你要是能站我这儿，像我这样看看你自己就好了。

……回想我们的身体如何像填字游戏中纵横交错的词语一样完美地融入彼此。

可你就像这冷冷的夜雨，满世界地下，你近在眼前，我却找不到你，

近不来
远不待
却无处不在

只当呼啸而过的车辆溅起水花，打湿我的裤腿——那一阵冰冷，才让我意识到自己的体温。雨点落向台阶下的水洼，惊起层层晕圈，它们无声、清晰，不断地走向消亡，我愣愣地望着圈中的自己，直到你从身后挽起我的手。

就像同心的圈在水面上晕漾开来——

　　一路上，拥挤的车流、刺眼的灯光，你的脑袋靠在我的肩上，失去了重量。鸣笛声不断地提醒我这慢慢长夜孕育的恶意，街灯黯淡，医院的红色十字在灯红酒绿中成了厄运的预兆。车里的收音机里响起悠扬的莫扎特，你稍稍挪了挪脑袋，拉紧了生日那天我送给你的风衣。

你的身边，尽是厄运、苦难
和摆满病床的房间
心灵有价，大可以物相换

　　酒店的落地窗外，是世界的缩影，我摘掉眼镜，便只觉大地如夜，星光点点。我回过头，想呼唤你的名字，却只见你扔掉了大衣，脱掉了鞋，弯着腰坐在床边，微微耷拉着脑袋，两眼痴痴地望着墙角的拖鞋。你的牺牲化作委屈，化作无从开口的话语，凝聚成你嘴角的痣，永远地沉默，永远地渴望着你的声音。

在目眩的高空——
大地上撒满星辰

它久久在她唇边
渴望着她的声线

　　我脱鞋上床，盘腿坐在你身后。我把脸贴在你的背上，倾听你心的跳动，仿佛它的节奏会把你的选择泄露。你选择失去什么？还是你都想拥有？只有玄关的灯亮着，沙土般的昏黄中，我怕你选择遗忘。

选择，曾是
你的选择
在失去
成为失去以前
我始终
活在你的遗忘中——
直到被遗忘的那天

　　——遗忘。

　　我捋起袖子，用力拉起你的毛衣，

不等你抬手便扯过你的头顶。你发出泄气般的呻吟，刚一撤力，你便倒在我的胸口。我听见静电的声音，噼啪声在我的手臂上跳跃，仿佛你不知所措的舞步。

静电的火星点点
像落遍我肌肤的舞步

“对不起，我有点失控——算是……情不自禁。”

……她露出如羞似歉的笑容，似在说：我也是情不自禁。

你发起高烧，我不知道你经历了什么——看见了什么。轻薄的纱衣无法掩饰你浑身的颤抖，你的身体依然散发着海的气息。

你要我说点什么。我拿起床头的书，为你念诗：

……它静静地躺在床头的小桌上，在风躁影乱、坐立难安的夜晚，你顺手将它拿起，让它为你低唱，哄你入睡。

为什么我爱你，先生？
因为
风，从不要求小草回答
为什么他经过
她就不能动摇。

天空一片褐色，没有一朵云。我的左边，是一片没有波浪的大海，远端，是一条渐渐远去、融入天空的海岸，醒目的是离岸不远处的一具黑影，它轮廓模糊，时时在变化，像熊熊燃烧的鬼火；右边，是一望无尽、没有人烟的沙漠，巨大、透明的荧幕从天上

我看见，一个
早已离我远去的梦

我发现，一条
渺远的岸线

……那是个美丽的故事，以荒无人烟、寸草不生的沙漠为背景，主人公是一位名叫幻景的王子。

挂下，长镜头，你熟睡的脸；你的眼角抽动，掀起一阵风，沙子钻进我的眼睛，唤醒温热的眼泪。我脚不停步，沿着漫长的直线艰难前行。

你步履轻盈地向我走来，两手藏在身后，低着头，隐形的线拉动着我，我的脚离开石路，踩上柔软的草地，忽而停住——

碧绿的草地，金黄的阳光，白色的路牌，茂密的树丛，天空，小径，云，你。

“送给你。”

你在我面前站定，两腿笔直，上身微微后仰，微微挺出了小腹。

我出其不意地把你亲吻，你睁大了眼睛，一瞬间红了脸，没等你的嘴唇恢复原状，我一左一右，亲吻你的脸。

亲完我就跑。你我之间，就像你的嘴唇一样柔软，我一下把你甩在十米开外，一下又被你追上。

我们一起跌倒在树下的草垫上，我趴着，你躺着，你的手依然紧紧抓住我的手腕——喘了三两口气，你才反应过来，“嗖”地把手收回，转过头来，你胸前的相机顺着你柔软的前

拉动我的，是一根隐形的线。

在我的世界，我描绘他的存在
从没有一丝懈怠
可我不知——
该在何处一笔而终，
墨尽手抬

他的嘴唇！
他的亲吻！
他的吻！

我的心，仍旧柔软
一如那天，我认定你
非我莫属

……两人一起跌倒在丛丛干草上，不禁放声大笑。他把折弯的银质衣架扔到一旁，将胳膊绕在她的腰间。那台小小的晶体管收音机从她的手中掉落。

胸滚落，跳跃，着地，没有人看见我们，我们目光交融，片刻——久久，然后放声大笑。

你的吟叹声♥萦绕不去，它的质感与我想象中鲸鱼的歌声相似。它让我觉得安心，却令我更感孤独。你沉沉睡去，紧裹着满是皱褶的被子，呼吸变得平稳，被汗水浸透的床单慢慢变冷，我想象着你的身体。

♥……在满是褶皱的白色被单下，在我们急促的呼吸间，它成了坦白似的吟叹。

我打开床灯，顺手拿起丢在床头柜上的毛衣。一个松脱的线头♥——一次暧昧的暗示；熟悉的香水味此刻才变得清晰，我仿佛从遥远的未来回到现在；我抬起一条腿，伸到你两腿之间——重量、柔软。

♥……它就像我最心爱的毛衣上一个松脱的线头，我忍不住拉扯的冲动——

我把你的毛衣像围巾一样绕在脖子上，拿起床头柜上的钱夹。

那张照片，我永远也不会忘记——

一次期限不明的缓刑♥——

♥悲伤将她包裹，
　　像长长的围巾；
　　她久久等待
　　一次小小的缓刑——

天空是泛黄的蓝色，树是黯淡的绿，男孩留着利落的短发，穿着白色的衬衫、棕色的短裤。阳光穿过大而浓密的树冠，轻轻落在男孩肩上。他旁若无人地跪坐♥在地，露出皙嫩的侧脸：略略噘起的嘴唇，挺拔的鼻梁，被风拨动的头发，低垂的眼睛。我的

♥他以他的方式，记下我所有的梦
　　所有看似残酷、依旧模糊的事物
　　在那扭曲的怪树下
　　一个美丽的姑娘双膝落地，久久跪下

目光循着他的视线，顺着他细长的手臂，停在他紧紧合捧的手上。

在他手心，一只蓝色的小鸟睁着好奇的眼睛，张开了柔弱的翅膀。

寂寞的车站，破败的旋转木马，夕阳的余晖和你的目光一起，阅读着泥土与石木，加深了伤感。光泽不再的木马已经停下，却显得异常清晰，低矮的小木门开着，没有音乐流淌。你出神地与一匹粉红的马儿对视，却仍轻轻眨眼，不似想起了什么，马儿不再奔跑，回忆也便定格在某个地方，落在地上。

夜幕落下，狭长的候车间里只有你我二人。你枕着我的大腿，弯着膝盖，睡在仿佛没有终点的长凳上。左手边是玻璃门，铁轨在十米开外，再远处是灌木，再远处是山，山外是海，海外是人间。左上方的墙上是老旧的钟，钟的上方是说不出形状的孤灯。我看着秒针，给自己十秒，用指尖抚过你额前的头发，你的身体在绒衣里一起一落，像不曾远去的海浪；灯光下，指针一长一短，屏气敛息，却无处可藏。

忽然，我猛地扭头——融入夜色

旋转的木马
　　搭载回忆
　　转个不停
　　模糊了光影

我拼命回忆
　　不断不停
　　却难再想起
　　当时的情景

你好吗，我的爱
　　你越过波涛汹涌的大海
　　远在危机四伏的人间

就像钟表
　　不知分秒

这是它们的
　　存在之道

的黑影，在昏暗中，长凳的尽头。

你的眼睛乍然睁开，风打着卷，无数枯叶染上深褐，从天上飘落。荧幕开始闪动，换帧，黑点闪现，你的眼神变得惊恐异常。

当我闭上双眼，那些光景化作蒙太奇式的模糊影像，一帧帧播放。

你的脸仍然充填着整个画面，压迫感，窒息，我的心濒临破裂。你像被无形之手掐住了脖子，你的双唇颤动，你瞪大了通红的眼睛，一眨不眨地望着远方的鬼火——它正慢慢沉入海中。

她翕动双唇
为之歌唱的船骸
意味着她
从未离开

我们潜入海中。海水冰冷刺骨。五彩的鱼儿围绕你我，你伸手寻求它们的身体，它们下意识地躲闪，不曾改变过方向，似乎早已习惯了诱惑，看透了情愁。你不断地寻觅，尝试，终而放弃，你伸出的手久久没有收回，软绵绵地漂在水中，无力地解释着你的初衷。

“你为什么把没有打结的网扔进水里？”女孩问。“我想捕到大海里所有的鱼，”渔夫回答，“可我不想把任何一条占为己有。”

我不停划动手臂，我的身体四十五度倾斜，向海底而去，你捏紧鼻子，鼓起耳膜，你的身体四十五度倾斜，往浅处升浮。我们重新遇见彼此，我们同时转头向左，潜水镜模糊了视线，可在陌生的大海中，那偶然的相认和彻骨的依恋，让你目光中的惊喜化作我心中的确信。那一瞬间，宿命的邂逅，鱼群消失，无从拯救的错过——逆向的重逢，无力，无法呼喊，暗流加速，无法留住你，可我同时觉得幸运，一种关于个人、关于艺术、关于梦、关于彼岸的、已在潜意识中销声匿迹的默契被重新唤醒。我像小草向往风儿、像海浪向往月光一样，对未来充满了憧憬。你在海底看见了什么？我看见坚硬的珊瑚，宛如记忆的细沙，残破的网，巨蟹，招展的海葵，透明的鱼像古老的灵感，海的咒语，光，海草在舞蹈，黑色的火焰拥抱船骸，纪念夭折的诗篇。

可你说你闯入了禁区，你说一切的不快、一切被懦弱压缩的时光，终于凝聚一处，化作那乌黑的海鸟，回头向你俯冲而来。你湿着头发，倒在我的怀里，满面苍白地挤出微笑，眼中是海的深蓝。

——你看见了什么？

在陌生人的海洋
　　你久久企盼，企盼与我相知

……那一次次微笑、一声声低语，无一不让我更加确信，确信一个不可能的结论：我曾认得你，也曾爱过你——

——曾经，在那个短暂的瞬间——我身裹你的怀抱，觉得自己那么幸运，那么、那么幸运。

……疯了似的寻找最初的你，寻找一切我已无从想起的细节——一切在潜意识中销声匿迹的细小回忆。

……那是像时间一样古老的咒语。

落向你的内心
　　不容你涉足的深处

……就像这辈子听见的每一声再见——在同一时间，传至耳边。

我手捧他双手的苍白
　　看见他笑里透蓝

我的望着长凳尽头的黑影——是谁？我瞪大了疲惫的双眼，呼吸仿佛获得了理由，你的身体仍然轻稳地起伏——

有个男人
来了又走
他曾是我
每一次呼吸的理由

木马转动起来，在我和黑影之间，粉色的灯一盏盏亮起，马背上空无一人，熟悉的音乐响起，稀薄的影像一点点升起，飘浮在半空，木马越转越快，渐渐模糊了光影。我的手捏紧袋里的书，将食指的指甲挤进书页——这里只有你我，谁又能了解我的秘密？我的手心渗出汗液，书硬得像砖，我冷得像冰。

……一些词句会脱离纸页，升浮入空……

毫无疑问
我必须阅读
阅读所有
在书中读到的书

一声汽笛如天使降临一般把我拯救，我转头望向门外，再回头，木马和黑影都已不在，你的鼻子、侧脸在我腿间揉蹭，你咿呀作声，慢慢醒来，我的呼吸再次失去了理由。

……他的出现，并不是为了拯救你，而是为了让你懂得如何去拯救自己。

火焰被海吞没，狂风咆哮，抚平了你眉间的皱褶，吹散了你脆弱的容颜，你听，海在低语——我踩着落叶冲向沙漠，不曾回头，风沙化作巨大的手，捏合破碎的影像，塑就明亮的街灯，在眼前，在远处。

听，我想你，是海在低语，风咆哮不止。

在爱情中
找到向导
不入迷途
不复心碎

我睁开眼睛，眼前是床灯的橘黄和空如大海的床单。

……空空的床单映入眼帘，宣告着又一次失去的开端。

那夜，你拿起床头的书，为我念诗：

我本可以忍受黑暗，

如果我不曾见过阳光。

可阳光早已不是阳光，阳光是翱翔在天空的蓝鸟，黑暗也不再是黑暗，黑暗是消失的漂流瓶，我不再是我，我是长凳尽头的黑影，爱也不再是爱——

爱就是你。

手不再是手，手是拥抱与爱抚；嘴也不再是嘴，它们变成亲吻。我的名字不再是一个名字，它是一声呼唤。爱也不再是爱——爱就是你。

叶紫

2018年9月28日

于鲁迅文学院

时北京风似想念、爱如红枫

『得不到，已失去』

爱已成诗

[澳]朗·丽芙◎著
叶紫◎译

浙江文艺出版社

图书在版编目（CIP）数据

爱已成诗 /（澳）朗·丽芙著；叶紫译．—杭州：浙江文艺出版社，2021.1
ISBN 978-7-5339-6216-6

Ⅰ．①爱…　Ⅱ．①朗…　②叶…　Ⅲ．①诗集—澳大利亚—现代　Ⅳ．①I611.25

中国版本图书馆 CIP 数据核字（2020）第 167932 号

爱已成诗
AI YI CHENG SHI
作　　者：［澳］朗·丽芙
译　　者：叶紫
责任编辑：诸婧琦
装帧设计：居居

出版发行：浙江文艺出版社
地　　址：杭州市体育场路 347 号
网　　址：www.zjwycbs.cn
经　　销：浙江省新华书店集团有限公司
印　　刷：浙江新华数码印务有限公司
开　　本：787 毫米 ×1092 毫米　1/32
印　　张：5.5
插　　页：1
版　　次：2021 年 1 月第 1 版
印　　次：2021 年 1 月第 1 次印刷
书　　号：ISBN 978-7-5339-6216-6
定　　价：42.00 元

FOR MICHAEL

The half of this book—
the whole of my heart.

致迈克尔

这部书，一半是你——
我内心的全部。